To my grandchildren, Jackson & Emme.

You inspire me each and every day!

www.mascotbooks.com

The United Forest of Kind

For more information, please contact:
Mascot Books
560 Herndon Parkway #120
Herndon, VA 20170
info@mascotbooks.com

Library of Congress Control Number: 2017908384

CPSIA Code: PBANG0817A
ISBN-13: 978-1-68401-354-8

Printed in the United States

The United
Forest of Kind

by Anne Grall Reichel

illustrated by Junica

It was early November in the United Forest of Kind.

Squirrel, a wise and kind creature of the forest, sat quietly on a branch of the old oak tree where she had built her nest and prepared for winter. She looked out over the forest.

Squirrel sensed that something was terribly wrong.

The fall had been unusually warm. The leaves still clung to the oak tree that Squirrel shared with many other creatures of the forest.

Squirrel's friends were not preparing for the winter. Instead of hiding acorns, gray squirrels spent the day chasing red squirrels as they tried to gather pinecones in the neighborhood.

Squirrel was puzzled!

Why would gray squirrels chase after pinecones when they would rather eat acorns? After all, plenty of acorns still clung to the branches of the old oak tree.

Squirrel thought about how the forest had changed.

In the past, all the animals would work side by side to prepare for winter. Now they were working against each other.

Robins, who passed through the United Forest of Kind on their journey to warmer forests, had decided to stay for the warm fall.

Squirrel was very upset when she noticed that other winter birds would not share their trees or food with the robins.

She wondered if the forest was no longer a kind place to live.

The next day, Squirrel noticed that Fox now ran long distances through neighborhoods where people and other animals lived, instead of crossing through the forest.

Squirrel scurried down from her branch and leaped across the fence line to speak to Fox.

Fox explained that Coyote had made it impossible for her to come into the forest. She feared he would not let her cross safely back into the neighborhood to reach her den.

Squirrel wondered how all these things could be happening in the forest she loved.

The United Forest of Kind had become anything but kind!

In early December, the snow was blowing, and the wind chill was very cold. Squirrel worried about her friends who were not prepared for the harsh weather.

By March, things were not any kinder. The spotted salamander who lived under a decaying log in the forest told Squirrel her worries about the journey across the fence to the neighborhood pond to lay her eggs.

Salamander feared that once her eggs hatched and her young made their miraculous change to salamanders, they would not be able to survive the journey back into the forest because of the dangers of crossing the fence line.

In the past, animals from the forest had always helped protect them. Now, everyone feared the fence line.

The dead trees that were home to insects, nesting holes for chickadees, and places for squirrels to store pinecones and nuts, were once great food sources for raccoons, opossums, and skunks to share.

Now, Squirrel watched as Skunk stood below the hollow tree and declared it was his tree. He lifted his tail to spray the raccoons and opossums every time they came to eat.

By spring, Squirrel was heartbroken. Wise, kind, gentle Squirrel found herself shouting as loud as she could, "This is INTOLERABLE!"

Squirrel knew the animals of the forest were better than this. They had always welcomed all creatures and been the United Forest of Kind.

Squirrel cried herself to sleep.

When she woke up, Squirrel began to problem-solve.

She realized that shouting out to the forest did little good and decided to lead the forest by example instead.

On day one, she gathered pinecones and acorns and invited the red and gray squirrels to the old oak tree to share dinner.

On day two, she collected food for the robins and winter birds to share.

On day three, she took Fox to speak to Coyote, explaining that there was plenty of food in the forest to be shared.

On day four, she convinced her forest friends to stay up late to ensure safe passage for the young salamanders across the fence line.

On day five, she helped
Skunk share the food
from the hollow trees with
Opossum and Raccoon.

Each day as Squirrel did her acts of kindness, she sang a song.

This little life of mine,

I'm going to live it kind!

This little life of mine,

I'm going to live it kind!

This little life of mine,

I'm going to live it kind!

Live it kind,

Live it kind,

Live it kind!

Animals who experienced Squirrel's kindness began doing kind acts too. They spoke up when they saw something that was not right.

Soon, the United Forest of Kind was returning to the values that made it great so long ago.

About the Author

Anne has enjoyed a fulfilling career as a science educator and teacher of teachers. She has taught a wide range of students from elementary to graduate level. She earned her doctorate in educational leadership with an emphasis on teaching for conceptual integration. She continues to do professional development of teachers on a limited basis.

Anne is a dedicated wife, mother, and grandmother. She enjoys precious time with her grandchildren, long walks with her husband, and finds solace in writing and gardening.

In recent years, Anne has become deeply concerned about the general lack of kindness, civility, and respect our children observe, from bullying in schools to political rhetoric. She has noticed that simple acts of kindness seem to be perceived as unexpected. She remembers when they were the norm.

Anne wonders if somewhere along the way, kindness became associated with weakness. She believes acts of kindness require strength, integrity, and a strong sense of self. Anne wrote this book because she believes that kindness is desperately needed in our turbulent world. She hopes the book holds messages for both children and adults.